1/08

Teen Minorities in Rural North America
Growing Up Different

Title List

Getting Ready for the Fair: Crafts, Projects, and Prize-Winning Animals

Growing Up on a Farm: Responsibilities and Issues

Migrant Youth: Falling Between the Cracks

Rural Crime and Poverty: Violence, Drugs, and Other Issues

Rural Teens and Animal Raising: Large and Small Pets

Rural Teens and Nature: Conservation and Wildlife Rehabilitation

Rural Teens on the Move:
Cars, Motorcycles, and Off-Road Vehicles

Teen Life Among the Amish and Other Alternative Communities:
Choosing a Lifestyle

Teen Life on Reservations and in First Nation Communities:
Growing Up Native

Teen Minorities in Rural North America: Growing Up Different

Teens and Rural Education: Opportunities and Challenges

Teens and Rural Sports: Rodeos, Horses, Hunting, and Fishing

Teens Who Make a Difference in Rural Communities: Youth Outreach
Organizations and Community Action

Teen Minorities in Rural North America
Growing Up Different

by Elizabeth Bauchner

Mason Crest Publishers

Philadelphia

Mason Crest Publishers Inc.
370 Reed Road
Broomall, Pennsylvania 19008
(866) MCP-BOOK (toll free)
www.masoncrest.com

First printing
1 2 3 4 5 6 7 8 9 10
ISBN 978-1-4222-0011-7 (series)

Library of Congress Cataloging-in-Publication Data

Bauchner, Elizabeth.
    Teen minorities in rural North America : growing up different / by
Elizabeth Bauchner.
        p. cm. — (Youth in rural North America)
    Includes index.
    ISBN 978-1-4222-0014-8
    1.   Minority teenagers—United States—Juvenile literature. 2.   Rural
youth—United States—Juvenile literature. 3.   Racism—United States—
Juvenile literature. 4.   United States—Race relations—Juvenile literature.
5. United States—Ethnic relations—Juvenile literature. 6. United States—
Rural conditions—Juvenile literature. I. Title. II. Series.
    HQ796.B333 2006
    305.235089'00973—dc22
                                                2005029386

Cover and interior design by MK Bassett-Harvey.
Produced by Harding House Publishing Service, Inc.
www.hardinghousepages.com

Cover image design by Peter Spires Culotta.
Cover photography by iStock Photography (Christine Glade).
Printed in Malaysia by Phoenix Press.

Contents

Introduction

by Celeste Carmichael

Results of a survey published by the Kellogg Foundation reveal that most people consider growing up in the country to be idyllic. And it's true that growing up in a rural environment does have real benefits. Research indicates that families in rural areas consistently have more traditional values, and communities are more closely knit. Rural youth spend more time than their urban counterparts in contact with agriculture and nature. Often youth are responsible for gardens and farm animals, and they benefit from both their sense of responsibility and their understanding of the natural world. Studies also indicate that rural youth are more engaged in their communities, working to improve society and local issues. And let us not forget the psychological and aesthetic benefits of living in a serene rural environment!

The advantages of rural living cannot be overlooked—but neither can the challenges. Statistics from around the country show that children in a rural environment face many of the same difficulties that are typically associated with children living in cities, and they fare worse than urban kids on several key indicators of positive youth development. For example, rural youth are more likely than their urban counterparts to use drugs and alcohol. Many of the problems facing rural youth are exacerbated by isolation, lack of jobs (for both parents and teens), and lack of support services for families in rural communities.

When most people hear the word "rural," they instantly think "farms." Actually, however, less than 12 percent of the population in rural areas make their livings through agriculture. Instead, service jobs are the top industry in rural North America. The lack of opportunities for higher paying jobs can trigger many problems: persistent poverty, lower educational standards, limited access to health care, inadequate housing, underemployment of teens, and lack of extracurricular possibilities. Additionally, the lack of—or in some cases surge of—diverse populations in rural communities presents its own set of challenges for youth and communities. All these concerns lead to the greatest threat to rural communities: the mass exodus of the post–high school population. Teens relocate for educational, recreational, and job opportunities, leaving their hometown indefinitely deficient in youth capital.

This series of books offers an in-depth examination of both the pleasures and challenges for rural youth. Understanding the realities is the first step to expanding the options for rural youth and increasing the likelihood of positive youth development.

CHAPTER 1
Growing Up Different: Issues and Challenges Faced by Minorities in Rural North America

E'Vonne Coleman, an African American artist from the rural South, grew up in the 1960s in North Carolina. "We were poor," she said in a speech to students at the University of Massachusetts, "But I did not feel it. We were *segregated*, and I could see it."

Coleman attended a school for African American children through the eighth grade, and then desegregation laws took hold and she attended an integrated high school. "We were all forced to merge my freshman year and it was different and confusing for many of us. We, the black

Prejudice and discrimination still exist throughout North America.

What's the Difference Between Prejudice, Discrimination, and Racism?

Prejudice is an attitude, opinion, or feeling formed without prior knowledge, thought, or reason. Discrimination literally means to discern between two seemingly different objects; however, it is also treatment that favors one individual or group over another. Racism is racial prejudice and discrimination supported by institutional power and authority for the advantage of one race over another. A critical element of racism is the use of institutional power and authority to support prejudice and enforce discriminatory practices.

students, were forced on the bus. And it was clear that we were not welcomed in the white schools."

The lessons her family gave her at the time were to stay out of trouble, do her work, and "mind the white folks," as *Jim Crow laws* were alive and well. Her family tried to instill in her how to belong in a dominant white culture. "We were taught that we must be three times better, three times brighter, three times smarter, three times more educated than our white counterparts in order to succeed in America," she said. "It was not enough that we were citizens."

Coleman said she was "saved by drama" in her high school, and later studied drama and sociology at North Carolina Central University. After graduation, she became the executive director of the National Endowment for the Arts (NEA) Expansion Arts program. Begun in 1971, Expansion Arts was established to fund projects and organizations deeply rooted in and reflective of inner-city, rural, and tribal communities.

According to Coleman, "Expansion Arts created a table where rural arts and multiculturalism co-existed." She wanted to help spread the idea that the arts are crucial to our lives, and that we can build community through our arts programs. She has since gone on to hold various positions in community service and business organizations, devoting much of her time to the arts.

Coleman's experience growing up in the segregated South was certainly not an isolated experience. Even today, many African Americans in rural America deal with racism and prejudice on a daily basis, in some ways much like Ms. Coleman did when she was younger. Although Jim Crow laws are no longer applicable, African Americans, as well as other minority populations, still face many barriers to education, work, and health care that have carried over from racist attitudes of the past. In this way, racism in many rural communities maintains its stranglehold on the minority populations who live there.

Who Are Rural Minorities?

Oftentimes when people think of minority populations, they think of inner cities and other urban areas, but actually, almost half the rural population in the United States is comprised of minority populations. These populations include African Americans, Native Americans (including American Indians, Inuit, and Aleuts), and Latinos. Two other large minority groups in North America are Asians and Pacific Islanders, but they mainly live in urban areas and will not be included in this book when the term "rural minority" is used in a general sense.

Almost half the U.S. rural population is comprised of minority populations.

What's in a Name?

Native American or American Indian? Hispanic or Latino? African American or black? What's in a name, anyway?

When Christopher Columbus landed in the Americas in 1492, he mistakenly believed he had landed in the East Indies, and so he called the natives of the land *Indians*. In recent years, many Americans have come to prefer the term *Native American* over *Indian*, both as a term of respect and as a correction to the **misnomer** Columbus bestowed on the native people. In Canada, the preferred term is *First Nation*. Many native groups, however, prefer to be called by their tribal name—Seneca, Osage, or Seminole, for example—or simply American Indian.

Though often used interchangeably in North America, "Hispanic" and "Latino" are not identical terms. Hispanic derives from the Latin word for "Spain" and is a broader reference, potentially encompassing all Spanish-speaking peoples in the world. Latino refers more exclusively to persons or communities of Latin American origin. Of the two, only Hispanic can be used in referring to Spain and its history and culture; a native of Spain residing in the United States is a Hispanic, not a Latino.

Names also carry with them a strong sense of identity. For a certain segment of the Spanish-speaking population, Latino is a term of ethnic pride and Hispanic is a label that borders on the offensive because white government officials gave it to them without asking them what they wanted to be called. According to this view, Hispanic lacks the authenticity and cultural resonance of Latino, since the word *Latino* has a more Spanish sound and can show the feminine form (Latina) when used for a woman.

Different terms for African Americans have also been used at various points in history, including Negroes, colored, blacks, and Afro-Americans. Negro and colored are no longer used and are now considered to be **derogatory** terms. African American, black, and to a

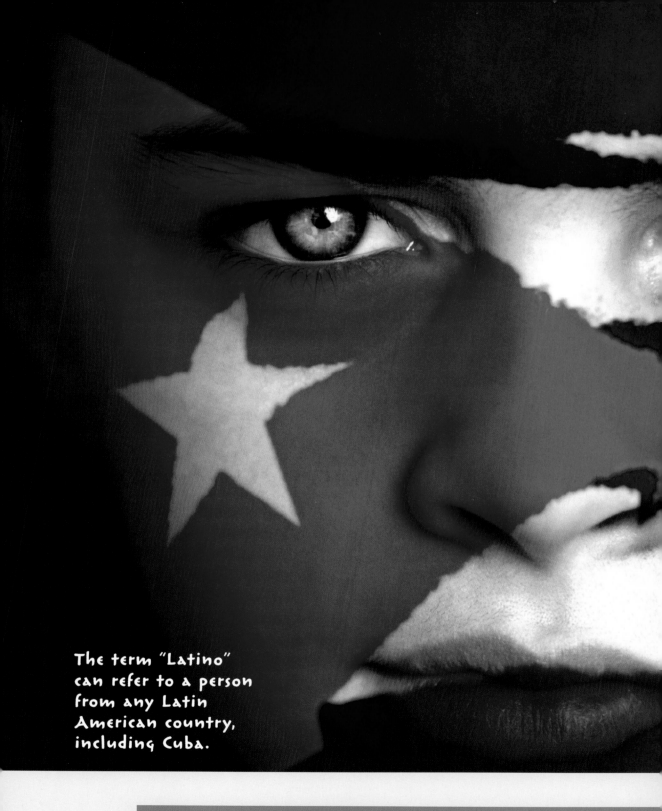

The term "Latino" can refer to a person from any Latin American country, including Cuba.

What Is a Rural Minority County?

Most counties in the United States are comprised of diverse groups of ethnic peoples, including whites. However, some counties are considered to be rural minority counties. In 1990, approximately 7.2 million minorities (half the rural minority population) lived in rural areas with a substantial or predominant minority population, meaning at least one-third of the population belonged to one minority group. Although the number of rural minority counties was small—333 rural minority counties out of 2,288 rural counties—the rural minority counties are important to note because of their disproportionately higher rates of poverty.

lesser extent, Afro-American, are used interchangeably today. The term African American, as originally coined, refers to the descendants of Africans who arrived in the United States as slaves; it generally does not refer to recent African immigrants, who usually adopt country-of-origin identifiers. However, the term properly can be applied to nearly all black citizens of the United States.

Poverty Is Higher Among Rural Minorities

A big problem facing rural minorities is extreme poverty. Poverty affects a person's life in many ways, from not having enough

Individuals of African descent are often referred to as African Americans. Many, however, prefer to be simply called "black." In some cases, black individuals are also Latinos, as is the case with this young man from Puerto Rico.

Native reservations are considered rural communities.

nutritional foods to eat, to not having access to health care and adequate housing, to living in areas with poorer public schools and lack of access to transportation and social services. While it's true that individuals respond differently to the challenges they face, people who live in extreme poverty have many more challenges to face than people who live in relative middle-class comfort.

Not all rural minorities live in poverty, but the numbers are still disproportionately higher for minorities than they are for whites, and also higher in rural areas than in metropolitan areas. For example, in the United States in 2000, the official poverty rate in non-metropolitan areas was 13.4 percent, whereas poverty in metropolitan areas was 10.8 percent. The national poverty rate among rural minority children is currently about 24 percent, much higher than the national poverty rate. On average, rural residents have higher unemployment rates and earn lower wages than urban residents.

Furthermore, rural poverty occurs mainly in isolated pockets, where deep poverty (annual incomes less than $7,500 per year) affects more of the population (as much as 40 percent of the people in a rural county). Poverty rates tend to be exceptionally high in rural counties in Appalachia, the Mississippi Delta, Native American reservations in the Southwest and Great Plains, the lower Rio Grande Valley in Texas, and the central valley of California. With the exception of Appalachia, most of these counties have large minority populations.

Rural Minority Populations: Past and Present

As most people are likely aware, the majority of the African American population in North America today had ancestors who were brought here from Africa to work as slaves. After *emancipation*, many African Americans stayed near the plantations where they had worked as slaves to work as *sharecroppers*. Because of the sharecropper laws and regulations, many African Americans couldn't afford to buy their own land, and that problem still affects today's rural African American population.

Today, most rural African American populations tend to be clustered in counties along the Mississippi Delta and other areas in the Deep South, including Louisiana and Alabama. Other rural primarily African American counties exist in southern Maryland and along the Virginia–North Carolina border.

Latinos are the fastest-growing rural minority population. In the past ten years, their numbers have more than doubled in rural areas. The largest Hispanic rural populations are along the Rio Grande, from its headwaters in southern Colorado to the Gulf of Mexico in Texas. Other dense populations live in the high plains of Texas and New Mexico.

Native Americans, who once lived all over the North American continent, are now fragmented across the landscape. Only about half of the Native American population lives in a rural area, and most of those rural areas are American Indian reservations far from metropolitan areas.

Community, Culture, Friendship, and Family

The rural minority groups in North America have a rich and varied past. Family, community, and culture are very important to Native Americans, African Americans, and Latinos alike. A sense of cultural identity is very important to many minorities as a counteragent against years of *oppression*. Parents and grandparents often have a strong desire to pass on their cultural beliefs to their children and grandchildren.

Values like family, community, and culture are very important to Native Americans, African Americans, and Latinos.

The quinceañero is an important rite of passage for many Latina girls. This celebration of a young woman's fifteenth birthday marks her entrance into womanhood. It is as big an event in her life as her wedding will be.

To celebrate and preserve cultural roots, Native Americans have many *rites of passage*, as well as celebrations that honor the Earth and sky. These celebrations include ritual foods and music, along with prayer and meditation. African American culture includes music, dance, a strong appreciation for the arts, a deep connection with family members, and strong religious beliefs. Many Latinos also have strong religious beliefs that guide many of their decisions and cultural celebrations.

Rural minority teens face many of the same issues that any other North American adolescent does—but their lives are also influenced by the unique cultures to which they belong. A look at each minority's culture and history is an important foundation for understanding these teens' strengths and challenges.

CHAPTER 2
Cultural Histories of Rural Minority Populations

History is not merely something that happened long ago. Each North American minority has its own story—and these stories still shape their lives today.

American Indians' Story

Long before European settlers arrived in the New World, many different Native tribes inhabited the North American continent. Most scholars believe these people came into the Western Hemisphere from Asia via the Bering Strait or along the North Pacific coast in a series of migrations, during the last ice age, between 20,000 and 30,000 years ago. From Alaska, they spread east and south.

You can learn more about Native American history and contemporary life at the National Museum of the American Indian, which opened in Washington, D.C., on the National Mall in 2004. There is also a museum in New York City and one in Maryland. If you can't go there in person, visit the Web site at www.nmai.si.edu/index.cfm.

At the time of Columbus's arrival in the fifteenth century, somewhere between 1.8 and 10 million Native Americans lived north of Mexico. These numbers include groups from several major cultural areas, including the Northwest coast, the Plains, the Eastern Woodlands, and the Southwest. There were also groups in the Arctic region, including Aleuts and Inuits.

These groups developed different lifestyles and social organizations depending on the region they inhabited and their available food sources. For example, the Northwest Indians, who lived along the thickly wooded, *temperate* Pacific Coast from southern Alaska to northern California, consumed salmon as their main source of food, and supplemented that with seals, sea lions, deer, and elk. They developed fishing and hunting techniques appropriate to the area, and they built houses and canoes out of wood.

In contrast, the Plains Indians, who lived both nomadic and sedentary lifestyles, made dome-shaped lodges surrounded by earthen walls, which the Northwest Coast Indians would never have been able to make due to the rainy climate of the Pacific Northwest. The Plains Indians lived in the grasslands between the foothills of the Rocky Mountains and the Mississippi River, from just north of the Canadian border south to Texas. The sedentary Plains people raised what is known as the "three sisters": corn, beans, and squash,

An 1884 photograph of a First Nations tribe in Quebec

Native American traditions influence how Native teens live today.

while those who were nomadic traveled on foot, slept in tepees, and hunted buffalo as their main food staple. They often traded buffalo meat and hides for corn, squash, and beans from the sedentary Plains Indians.

Some Native Americans developed formal social *hierarchies* and complex forms of government. For example, the Eastern Woodlands Indians—which included the Natchez, Choctaw, Cherokee, and Creek Indians who lived in what is now the eastern part of the United States from the Atlantic Ocean to the Mississippi River, and also in the Great Lakes region—developed elaborate social structures and large villages headed by chiefs. Their societies were often divided into classes, with a chief, his children, nobles, and commoners. Like the sedentary people of the Plains, the Eastern Woodland Indians also grew corn, beans, and squash; and they hunted deer.

These people spoke many different languages; created many different forms of artwork, music, and basketry; believed many different creation stories; and held different ceremonies. One thing they had in common was that the Europeans took over their land and eventually moved them onto reservations. In some cases, Native Americans were murdered and tribes were completely wiped out, while others remain today and are trying to piece together what's left of their language, culture, and heritage.

According to the 2000 U.S. Census, approximately half of all Native Americans live in rural areas today. The largest tribes in the United States (by population) are Cherokee, Navajo, Choctaw, Sioux, Chippewa, Apache, Blackfoot, Iroquois, and Pueblo. The 2003 U.S. Census Bureau estimates a little more than one-third of the 2,786,652 Native Americans in the United States live in three states: California, Arizona, and Oklahoma.

Whether positively or negatively, Indians' history influences their current life. Native Americans' experience of the last 500 years includes military defeat, cultural pressure from Europeans, confinement on reservations, forced cultural assimilation, the outlawing of Native languages and culture, and forced sterilizations. As recently as the 1960s, Indians were being jailed for teaching their traditional beliefs. During the 1970s, the **Bureau of Indian Affairs** was still actively pursuing a policy of "*assimilation*," the goal of which was to eliminate Indian reservations and steer them into mainstream U.S. culture.

There is no way to tell for certain just how much U.S. policy toward Native Americans has had a cumulative effect on their mental and physical health; however, contemporary mental health problems for Native Americans include high rates of alcoholism, depression, and suicide. Native Americans who live on reservations generally live the farthest away from urban areas and have little access to jobs that can help them out of poverty. Many of their native cultures have fallen apart or disappeared altogether.

African Americans' Story

Most African Americans in North America are descendants of sub-Saharan West Africans who were brought to the United States to work as slaves. Africans were shipped to the New World via slave ships over what is known as the "Middle Passage," a treacherous journey from West Africa to America, in which many Africans died along the journey from disease or maltreatment. The slave trade began in 1607 and lasted until the middle of the nineteenth century. By 1860, about 3.5 million blacks were enslaved in the South, and approximately 500,000 free blacks lived throughout the United States.

During slavery, blacks were forced to work the land on plantations in the South, as well as perform domestic service for white slaveholders and their families. Hundreds if not thousands of cases of abuse—including whippings, murders, and rapes—are documented. A customary practice was to sell slaves' loved ones, including their

Blacks were considered property whose purpose was to perform manual labor for white people; their humanity was not recognized, and they suffered many cruelties.

In the early twentieth century, the Ku Klux Klan marched proudly along the streets of the nation's capital.

children, at slave auctions. For over 250 years, this system of abuse based on race continued, instilling in many blacks a deep fear and loathing of the white race.

After the end of the Civil War in 1865, however, the newly emancipated African Americans enjoyed relative freedom for the first time. This brief period of time, known as "Reconstruction" and lasting only until 1877, was marked by the growth and development of many African American communities, including churches, schools, and businesses. African American men won the right to vote, and many of them were given prominent positions in government, including state senators and legislators. However, this period of hope and progress ended when Southern whites, still angry over their loss in the Civil War, found new ways to *disenfranchise* blacks.

One of the ways that Southern whites rebelled against the emancipation of blacks was to pass a series of laws segregating nearly all public places, including theaters, railway cars, and places of employment. Often of inferior quality, hospitals, public schools, and other public institutions were created separately for blacks. These laws became known as Jim Crow laws.

Outright violence and terrorism were other means of intimidating and disenfranchising blacks. During the period after Reconstruction, the Ku Klux Klan was formed by former Confederates to reassert white *supremacy* through terrorism. The KKK was responsible for a violent wave of *lynchings* throughout the South.

Laws were also passed that prevented former slaves from purchasing land and owning businesses. Many former slaves ended up working as sharecroppers, doing some of the same work they did as slaves, supposedly to earn a paycheck. Due to the sharecropping scheme developed by white plantation owners, sharecroppers were allowed to "borrow" money to work their own plots of land and pay back the plantation owners at high rates of interest. In general, however, they never made enough to cover the loans and save enough to purchase land. The effect was that they remained in much the same position they had been as slaves.

The conditions in the South after Reconstruction sparked a huge migration of blacks in the early twentieth century to Northern states and to cities such as Chicago and Detroit, but many African Americans remained in rural areas of the South. Eventually, persistent racism in the South also led to the civil rights movement of the 1950s and 1960s.

In the 1990s and early twenty-first century, a reverse migration has taken place, as many African Americans from Northern cities move back to rural areas in the South. Today, while poverty is still higher among African Americans than it is for whites, many blacks enjoy improved social and economic standing. After the civil rights movement, a strong, vibrant, black middle class emerged in the United States and Canada. Collectively, however, African Americans remain at an economic, educational, and social disadvantage relative to whites.

Latinos' Story

Hispanics are an ethnic group, not a racial group. Hispanics can be any race, and most of them identify themselves as white on U.S. government forms. In the United States, Hispanics are the largest ethnic minority and the largest minority population currently moving from urban to rural areas. Their history in North America is as diverse as the Hispanic people, and varies according to the areas from which they emigrated.

Like Native Americans, Hispanics do not have one culture all their own; they are from Spain, Mexico, Cuba, the Caribbean, Peru, Brazil, Argentina, and every other Central and South American country. Thus, when they arrive in North America, they bring with them many diverse customs.

About two-thirds of Latinos in North America today are recent immigrants; either they or their parents moved here. However,

Many Latinos emigrate from their countries to find better opportunities in North America.

Teens who are recent immigrants to the United States may have to overcome a language barrier to succeed in school.

Hispanic history in the United States predates the founding of the country. After all, the Spanish were some of the first settlers in the New World.

The Spanish established St. Augustine, Florida, in 1565 and Santa Fe, New Mexico, around 1609. Spain ruled much of what is now the southwestern United States, as well as Central and South America until the mid-nineteenth century. Mexico won independence from Spain in 1821, and Texas from Mexico in 1836. When the United States signed the Treaty of Guadalupe Hidalgo with Mexico in 1848, the United States acquired the land that would later become Arizona, California, New Mexico, Nevada, Utah, and parts of Colorado and Wyoming. The Mexicans living in these areas became U.S. citizens and created the core of the nation's Hispanic population.

Not many Latinos moved to the United States when it was a new country. Also, very few Mexicans and other Latinos expanded beyond their settlements in the American Southwest. In 1820, the first year that immigration statistics were kept, only 178 people emigrated from Latin America, compared to more than 8,000 immigrants from mostly European countries.

In the second half of the twentieth century, a wave of immigrants from Mexico and other Latin American countries greatly increased the U.S. Hispanic population. Many immigrants arrived from Cuba when Fidel Castro gained power and Cuba became politically unstable. Civil wars and political upheaval in their native countries, and the promise of work and educational opportunities in the United States began to lure more immigrants from Latin America. These continue to be core reasons why Latinos relocate to the United States today.

Although the population of Hispanics in North America is larger today than ever before, Hispanics also played a large role in U.S. history. They have fought in every war from the Revolutionary War to the war in Iraq today. They also taught the European settlers in the American Southwest irrigation and mining techniques, and influenced architecture in the Southwest. Many of their building techniques are particularly well suited to the dry climate and land, and still inspire architects today.

Like other minority populations in rural areas, Latinos have disproportionately higher rates of poverty relative to whites. They also have the highest high school drop-out rates among all minorities. Many researchers believe this disparity has more to do with language and cultural barriers than outright racism, since most Latinos are recent immigrants and speak only Spanish at home, making the transition to U.S. schools more difficult, as they have to learn English in addition to reading, writing, and arithmetic.

How Does History Affect Youth Minorities Today?

Unfortunately, some of the hatred, intolerance, and violence shown toward minority populations in the past remains today—especially in rural areas where white supremacist organizations like the Ku Klux Klan still exist and actively recruit new members. These attitudes trickle down to the children of both white and minority families and influence their ideas about themselves and people who are different from themselves.

For some minorities, their ethnicity and race are a source of pride, and their families and cultural identity are rooted strongly in their history. Others are content to live a contemporary "American" life and have assimilated into the dominant white culture.

However people choose to lead their lives, history always plays a crucial role in who we are today. Understanding the roots of racism, for instance, can help eliminate it. And understanding the stories of people different from ourselves can help us accept others and live in a more peaceful world.

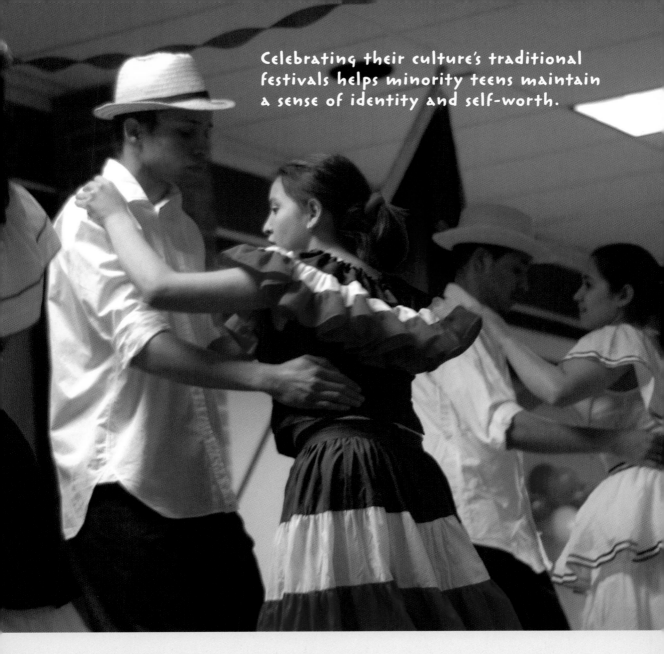

Celebrating their culture's traditional festivals helps minority teens maintain a sense of identity and self-worth.

Unfortunately, despite a growing awareness and acceptance of ethnic diversity by many in today's society, hate crimes and racial violence persist, especially against black people. Each time a hate crime happens, it offers reminders of a brutal past.

CHAPTER 3
Racism and Prejudice in Rural Areas

In the early morning hours of June 7, 1998, James Byrd Jr., a black man from Jasper, Texas, was walking home from an anniversary party when three white men in a pickup truck stopped and offered him a ride. After driving up a logging road deep into the woods, they got out of the truck. The three white men beat Byrd and chained him to the back of the truck. They dragged him behind the truck for nearly three miles before dumping his dismembered body in front of an African American church.

The horrifying murder sparked outrage across the world, and the three men who committed the crime—John William King Jr., Lawrence Russell Brewer Jr., and Shawn Allen Berry—were all charged with murder. Two of the men were associated with white supremacist groups such as the Ku Klux Klan, and the case brought to light the gruesome reality of racial violence, hatred, and intolerance in rural America.

Jasper is a small town in eastern Texas, about 45 percent black. Before Byrd's murder, African Americans held high positions in government and business. Jasper had a black mayor and a black hospital administrator. Residents of Jasper—both white and black—were shocked and saddened by the crime to James Byrd Jr.

How Racism Affects Minority Children

When racial violence hits or escalates, the effects are often devastating, not just to the individual victim and his family but to the entire community. People of color may experience feelings of fear, isolation, frustration, and anger following incidents of racially motivated hate crimes.

Children and adolescents are perhaps the most affected by racial violence and racism. Research shows that children who are exposed to violence—either as witnesses or as victims—often suffer immediate and sometimes long-term effects on mental health. Furthermore, minority children who are victims of racist attitudes, remarks, and bullying often experience symptoms of depression, low self-esteem, and other forms of psychological distress as a direct result of racism.

In 2003, a forum was held in Calgary, Alberta, to discuss how racism affects black people in Canada. Out of eighty-five participants, most expressed high levels of stress related to racism. Many found it harder to find jobs, even though they were well-educated; others found it hard to find housing (one woman was told that an apartment had been rented, but when she asked her white friend to call, the landlord told her it was still available); and others expressed

The psychological effects of racism are most devastating for children and adolescents.

Racism makes the lives of rural minority teens more difficult; it impacts their lives socially, emotionally, educationally, and even physically.

frustration with the school systems, claiming their children had been victims of racial taunts and bullying, and that the schools weren't doing anything about it. Some parents had even pulled their kids out of school to homeschool them because the classroom had become too stressful for their children.

Most important of all was the notion that racism in general made their lives more difficult than necessary, causing undue psychological stress and impairing their mental health. The participants spoke of how since childhood, white authority figures had told the participants they were not good enough, not smart enough, and did not behave well enough. The more a child hears this, the more likely he is to internalize the statements and begin to believe them.

Racism in Rural Areas

Unfortunately, the KKK and other white supremacist organizations like it flourish in rural areas, where economic conditions are often hard on everyone, including whites. Whites tend to resent any *upward mobility* by blacks or Hispanics. While it is doubtful that the KKK encouraged that particular crime—the three men who murdered Byrd seemed to do it on a whim—it is still unlikely their "whim" would have happened if the KKK hadn't influenced them.

Although white supremacist organizations are more visible in rural areas, their outright hatred and intolerance of nonwhite races and ethnicities is only one form of racism. Racism is not shown only through outward acts of violence. "Institutionalized" or "structural" racism also exists, and may be considered just as *insidious* and cruel as outward acts of racial-based violence.

Institutionalized racism is the process of purposely discriminating against certain groups of people through the use of biased laws or practices. Often subtle and manifesting itself in seemingly *innocuous* ways, its effects can be devastating. With institutionalized racism, many white people—who otherwise wouldn't consider themselves racist—participate unwittingly in discrimination against blacks or other minorities.

For example, many banks will routinely charge minorities a higher percentage rate for home loans than they charge white people. Individual loan officers may not think of themselves as racist, but they will still perpetuate the system of discrimination against minorities by enforcing the bank's policies.

Other examples of institutionalized racism can be found throughout history and in contemporary times. A great example comes from Beverly Daniel Tatum, an expert on race relations. In an interview for the Public Broadcasting System (PBS), she explains how just after World War II in the 1950s, the U.S. government offered veterans low-interest home loans as part of the GI Bill. The United States built millions of new homes in that decade, helped along by the encouragement of the government. However, just about all of those new homes were in the suburbs, and realtors, bankers, and others steered white people toward the nice, new white neighborhoods while attempting to keep black people in the older, urban neighborhoods or in rural areas.

The results of these racist policies and practices are still felt. The white veteran who received a low-interest loan from the government and moved to the suburbs—where there were better public schools and more *amenities* for raising kids—indirectly benefited from racist policies. As the children of these neighborhoods grew up, and their homes went up in value, and their fathers were able to put them through college, they worked hard, bought a house, and passed their wealth to their children. A generation or two down the line, and the beneficiaries of these earlier racist policies can't really see that they are privileged because of their race. It just seems "normal" or "how things are." That's the invisibility of structural racism.

In rural areas, this structural racism may not be so subtle. Segregation still openly exists in many parts of the rural South. It may not be legal, yet it persists.

Segregated schools contributed to institutionalized racism.

The Roots of Racism

Racism can be traced back to the slave trade and eighteenth- and nineteenth-century European ideas about the "inferiority" of African people. For Europeans to justify their capture and enslavement of African people, they had to think of the Africans as less than human. But what makes this attitude continue today? How did racism get passed from generation to generation? Why do some whites still think of themselves as superior to other races?

Research shows that parents are the earliest and most powerful source of racial attitudes—either positive or negative—with peers running a close second. By age two, a child notices color differences, and in the next two to four years, the child begins to identify with his or her own racial group. By the early elementary grades, every child carries at least some stereotyping of racial groups.

You might think that if parents are racist or pass on racist viewpoints, their children will be more likely to be racist as well. It does not always work out this way, however. Sometimes a child of racist parents grows up to befriend people of all races—or even marry someone of another race. Other times, children of nonracist parents grow up to be racist. Attitudes and opinions are formed through a variety of means.

For example, sometimes a child develops more racist attitudes from his peers. According to Jack Levin and Jack McDevitt in a report on hate crimes, adolescents and young adults are the most likely people to commit hate crimes. Sometimes, a person who doesn't hold any outright hatred for a racial group will commit a hate crime against a person of a particular race in order to impress his peers or belong to a peer group. Once the crime is committed, however, the perpetrator will then develop a racist attitude in order to justify his crime.

Of course, parents and peers aren't the only ones who help children develop attitudes about people of other races. Television and

An 1854 engraving depicts a black man being inspected for sale.

Multicultural education is important because it teaches children to respect others.

movies help reinforce the notion that "white" culture is the "norm," and, by extension, "better." This can easily translate into the idea that anyone who isn't white is somehow "not normal" or "bad," and both whites and minorities can come to believe this. The media plays a large role in most children's lives. If these children also happen to have parents who, for example, condemn black people for "preferring to live off welfare" and then that attitude is reinforced by television shows and news programs, their worldview is being shaped by the idea that white people are normal and good, and other races aren't.

Is Racial Harmony Possible?

If parents and peers can have such a huge impact on how children develop ideas about race, is it possible to help those children develop positive ideas about racial differences? Many schools in the United States and Canada are implementing multicultural programs to help children develop positive attitudes toward people of different races. What children need, according to one educational expert, are positive stories about people of different races.

In Texas, Clara Taylor, James Byrd's sister, is a middle-school teacher and proponent of multicultural education. She explained in an interview that the young men who killed her brother did, in fact, get a kind of education. "They didn't get that way overnight," she said, referring to the fact that the two men with ties to the KKK learned about the group and became affiliated with it while in prison for other crimes. Their "teachers" were, unfortunately, other criminals and white supremacists.

Taylor believes that the roots of racism are ignorance and hatred—and ignorance is something we can counteract by teaching students about people of other races. Hatred and racism take root,

When students in rural areas go to school with others from a variety of ethnic backgrounds, they have the opportunity to learn each other's stories. As understanding of each other is increased, ignorance, fear, and prejudice fade.

she explains, when people can't see anything connecting them to people of other races. One way to connect people to others is to give them stories that allow them to identify with each other's reality. That is a big part of what multicultural education is all about. The more we understand people who seem different from us, and the more we see the threads that connect us to others, the more likely we are to understand them, let go of our ignorance and fear, and be able to live in peace with many different people.

Many people are working to combat racism in both rural and urban schools. In addition to multicultural education, they also fight against racist policies (structural racism) that have made rural schools in minority counties some of the poorest schools in North America.

CHAPTER 4
Educational and Work Opportunities for Rural Minorities

In the fall of 2000, Stephen Sanchez, New Mexico's director of curriculum, instruction, and learning technologies, introduced online Advanced Placement (AP) courses to hundreds of high school students around the state who otherwise might not have had access to advanced studies.

"We're actually a 'minority majority' state," Sanchez said in an interview with Tech Learning, referring to the fact that in New Mexico, the majority of the population are Latinos and Native Americans living in rural communities. Not surprisingly, most of the students targeted for these online courses are Latinos and Native Americans.

55

The courses offer minority students in poorer communities a chance to learn the technology of computers while taking advanced classes in science, math, and English. "Underserved kids are hungry for advanced coursework," says Sanchez, "[but] without that opportunity, they lose their potential."

How Education Differs in Rural Communities

We've come a long way from the days when E'Vonne Coleman entered school for the first time with white students in her rural North Carolina high school. However, change happens more gradually than many of us would like, and disparities in the educational system between rural and urban areas exist, in part due to economic factors, which are, in part, a result of racism.

Teaching and learning don't happen in an isolated bubble; they happen within the social, cultural, political, environmental, and economic contexts of a particular place. These contexts influence the opportunities students have to learn and what the adults in their lives expect of them.

Although the contexts are interrelated, studies show a more direct relationship between a community's employment opportunities and the quality of schooling available. When major employers need an educated workforce, they tend to support quality schooling. This support is reinforced by the participation of educated parents. However, when local employment opportunities are insufficient, those who are well educated tend to leave the area. The community then loses its investment in education.

Historically speaking, most poor rural communities developed within economic conditions set by outside forces that used the community as a cheap labor source. For example, in Appalachia, the production of tobacco relied heavily on poor farmers while most of

A teacher in a rural school in Nunavut, Canada's northern province, works with First Nation students.

Nettie Hunt and her daughter, Nikie, sit on the steps of the U.S. Supreme Court in 1954.

the tobacco (and revenue) left the county. In slave- and sharecropper-based economies in the rural South, African Americans picked cotton for business owners who kept all or most of the profits, without reinvesting it in the local school systems.

Inequality and outside control of the community's resources have left many minority communities with low-performing educational systems and low expectations for students from poor families. Schools are asked to prepare students for jobs that are not available locally, and resources are often controlled by outsiders or local leaders who rely on access to a cheap labor force.

Brown v. the Board of Education

In 1954, the U.S. Supreme Court passed the landmark ruling that public schools could not segregate students based on race. The central question the Court addressed was whether segregation of children in public schools actually deprives minority children of equal educational opportunities. The Court ruled that such segregation is indeed harmful and went on to abolish the laws *requiring* segregation in seventeen states and *permitting* segregation in four other states. Many Southern states, such as North Carolina where E'Vonne Coleman lived, resisted the Court's decision until the 1960s.

The process of desegregation was difficult, and many states found ways around the new laws. Desegregation was mainly accomplished through closing the black schools and busing the black students to previously all-white schools. This system caused considerable conflict in many school districts, sometimes resulting in violence. Some school districts in Virginia closed for a year, others closed for several years while state-funded, private white schools flourished.

As time wore on, school districts found other ways of keeping black children from participating in a full spectrum of educational opportunities. After desegregation, a process called "tracking" developed that many black parents felt was segregation within the schools via course assignments and "ability grouping." Patterns developed in which low-income minority children experienced initial learning difficulties, sometimes as early as kindergarten, and were evaluated as "low-ability" and placed in low-track, remedial, or special education programs. By the time these children reached high school, they had never been given the full range of educational opportunities, having always been placed in low-track courses. If they stayed in school at that point, they were more likely than white children to be enrolled in vocational and general programs, whereas white children were mostly enrolled in higher academic programs.

Helping Rural Minority Students Succeed in School

Like the online AP courses in New Mexico, many pioneers in rural minority education are working on solutions to help students achieve educational goals, reduce the drop-out rate among poor rural minorities, and help these students go on to college. Other educators question if simply having access to advanced coursework is enough.

Research suggests that minority students benefit the most by having teachers and role models from their own race or ethnicity. When school desegregation took place in the rural South and the black schools closed, those black children also lost their black teachers, who were staunch advocates for their education. Many Southern schools have never recovered from their loss of African American teachers since the 1960s. Today, most minority students are taught by white teachers, who may or may not have any understanding of minorities' educational needs.

Research suggests that minority students benefit most by having teachers from their same race.

The Indian Boarding School Reversal: Akwesasne Freedom School

In the nineteenth century, the U.S. government created boarding schools for Indian children designed to force them to assimilate into mainstream American culture. Canada followed suit as well. According to Amnesty International, the boarding schools had a long history of abuse of the pupils. Many students died from malnutrition and disease, others were raped or forced to work as indentured servants to white families, and all of them were stripped of their cultural heritages, their native languages, and taken from their families.

In 1979, just as the Indian boarding school system was ending, the Mohawks—part of the Iroquois Nation—opened the first Native American school run by Native Americans. Located near the St. Lawrence River in upstate New York and Canada, the school is called Akwesasne Freedom School and is open to students in grades pre-K through eighth grade. Akwesasne, which means "the land where the partridge drums," teaches reading, writing, math, history, and science, as well as the Mohawk ceremonial cycle. Since 1985, all courses have been taught in the Mohawk language. Akwesasne fully immerses children in their native language. The ultimate goal is to preserve Mohawk language and culture, which was at risk for disappearing as native speakers died. The school has inspired other Native American tribes to open similar schools.

Tom Porter, the Mohawk chief for the Bear Clan (his Mohawk name is Sakokwenionkwas), explained:

The Germans can jump into the melting pot. The Swedish can jump in the melting pot. The Czechoslovakians can jump in there. The Polish can jump in there, too. But if some day those different nationalities all lose their language as they jump in the melting pot of America, if someday their grandchildren want to learn it, even if they have lost it, the Swedes can go back to Sweden, The Italians can go back to Italy, the Polish can go back to Poland, and they can regain their language that way. But where does the Mohawk go? There is nowhere in the world for other Iroquois to go if they want again to speak their language.

The sign for the Native boarding school in Tuba City, Arizona; although Indian boarding schools have a negative history, today they are run by the tribes, allowing them to become places where rural Native kids can be immersed in their cultures and languages.

TUBA CITY BOARDING SCHOOL • ESTABLISED 189 ELEMEMTARY & JR. HIG DEPT

In an article on rural African Americans and education, author Patricia Kusimo advocates for educators to go beyond teaching basic academic skills to "engaging students in critical reflection about realities such as social injustice." She explains that as a black student in a segregated school, she was told she would have to be twice as good as whites to succeed, and to expect some racism and bigotry when she started attending white schools. The overall message, however, was that she and her black peers could "fight back" through being excellent students.

Today, according to Kusimo, many African American students seem to believe the opposite. They see the school establishment as oppressive, and as they devalue high achievement standards, they inadvertently limit themselves. Other African American students, however, respond in the opposite way, citing their awareness of racism as a reason to excel, as Kusimo was taught as a young student. However, the African American teachers who communicated those messages to black children have diminished in number—and many black students are not getting the message that academic achievement is achievable or even all that desirable. Kusimo argues that there is a pressing need for teachers to carry the message that academic excellence is both "possible and essential for rural black students."

Reaching High Academic Achievement

In California there is a large population of Latino migrant farmworkers—the people who pick most of the foods distributed throughout the United States and Canada. Students in those families often must change schools three or even four times a year as their families move from farm to farm and follow different growing seasons. The students are often at risk for dropping behind in their

When children of migrant workers can't make it to the classroom, distance-learning programs bring the classroom to them.

studies—and eventually, dropping out altogether because of their frequent moves.

The Fresno Unified School District has addressed this problem by creating "Cyber High," an online high school available to anyone with computer access. It is aimed mainly at the children of migrant farmworkers, though it also now serves homeschooled children and adult learners. The program allows children who move frequently to complete coursework without having to go to class. Recent studies show that it boasts a 42 percent higher graduation rate for its students, as compared to other similar programs.

As Sanchez, the New Mexico educator, points out, students must be given opportunities to succeed or they risk losing their potential. Much research is being done in how communities can help their students. Sometimes, helping a student graduate high school takes more than coursework or even positive role models of the same race or ethnicity; sometimes it also takes access to nutritional foods, a healthy lifestyle, and adequate health care.

CHAPTER 5
Health-Care Issues for Rural Youth Minorities

In 1942, a young Latino man living in southern, rural California graduated from the eighth grade and began a full-time job as a migrant farmworker. He had already been working in the fields long before graduation. Migrant farmwork required many moves from farm to farm, wherever the farm contractors sent him and his family. By the time he had finished middle school, he had attended more than thirty schools.

This young man—César Chávez—never went beyond the eighth grade, although education became an important part of his life, and he valued it very much. After his formal schooling ended, Chávez continued to work the fields of California's southern and Imperial Valley. In 1944, at the age of seventeen, he enlisted in the Navy and served in World War II in the western Pacific. When he returned to the States, he also returned to migrant farm life.

In the 1940s and throughout the 1950s, migrant farmworkers, mostly Latinos, struggled with some of the harshest working and living conditions. Often entire families went to work, including small children. The only drinking water they had was what they were able to bring along for the day. Pickers had to bend over all day. The crops were often dusted or sprayed with pesticides that made many workers ill. They worked long hours and were not always paid what they had been promised. Most of the workers only spoke Spanish, however, so they could not argue their case well.

Chávez, who had been working in the fields since he was ten, had been observing the workers' plight all along. He learned English so that he could find out more about the farm contractors. He learned that many of them were *unscrupulous* and that there were virtually no laws to protect the rights of agricultural workers.

After the war, Chávez married another migrant farmworker, and they moved to San José. Soon after, he got involved in a community organization and began registering voters. Chávez read about politicians and civic leaders who used nonviolent means to accomplish change. He strongly believed that migrant farmworkers needed an organization to help them, and in 1962, with his own small savings, he formed the National Farm Workers Association, which later became the United Farm Workers (UFW).

César Chávez went on to bring awareness to the migrant farmworkers' difficult situation, and he succeeded in accomplishing many tasks. He helped organize a *boycott* of California table grapes in the 1960s, and he helped farmworkers when they went on strike for better working conditions. Many of these tactics resulted in better working conditions for farmworkers, but today much remains to be done.

Migrant workers face hard working conditions and unstable job situations.

Many children and adolescents become migrant farmworkers because their parents are migrant farmworkers.

The UFW still exists and offers migrant farmworkers the only *pension plan* available to them. The UFW also publishes reports on the state of migrant farmworkers and organizes action alerts so consumers can help support their cause.

Children and Adolescents as Migrant Farmworkers

Many migrant farmworkers begin working in the fields on a full-time basis when they were twelve years old or younger. A report by Human Rights Watch estimates that there are currently between 300,000 and 800,000 child farmworkers under the age of sixteen in the United States. (These numbers include children who work on family farms, although they are a small percentage.) The U.S. General Accounting Office admits there may actually be even more child and adolescent migrant farmworkers, but it concludes there is no accurate way to know for sure.

Children get involved in migrant farmwork because their parents are farmworkers. The average pay for a dual-earner family is approximately $14,000 per year, meaning individual workers make about $7,000 per year—far below poverty level. The children start working in the fields because their parents don't make enough money to support the family.

Health Concerns for Young Migrant Farmworkers

By far, the biggest concerns for adolescent migrant farmworkers involve health protection and health care. Children and adolescents working in the fields are afforded little protection, as current U.S.

Sometimes migrant farmworkers die from pesticide exposure, like seventeen-year-old Jose Antonio. In 1997, he was sprayed with pesticides from a tractor in the field where he worked. A week later, he was soaked again. After the second exposure, he became violently ill, showing symptoms of severe pesticide poisoning that included nausea, vomiting, sweating, diarrhea, and headaches. The next day, while riding his bike, he collapsed near his home in rural Utah. Emergency workers found white foam streaming from his nose, indicating pesticide poisoning. Rarely, if ever, are farm owners punished for these incidents.

law exempts agricultural businesses from many child labor laws. In other industries, strict laws dictate how many hours per day or week adolescents can work; in agriculture, however, children can work any amount of hours their bosses deem necessary, with only a few restrictions. Unfortunately, despite Chávez's gains in farmworker rights, virtually no laws protect child farm laborers.

Long working hours hinders their development. What's more, children are more vulnerable to pesticide exposure. Every year, physicians as well as groups like Human Rights Watch and the UFW hear frequent reports of migrant youths suffering from pesticide poisoning. Even if a child does not suffer immediate effects from pesticide exposure, long-term consequences may include leukemia, kidney tumors, brain tumors, brain damage, and learning and memory problems.

Migrant farmworkers do not have permanent residences; they move from farm to farm, following the crops, living in the facilities provided for them by the farm owners. As a result, workers often lack access to clean water and adequate sanitation. The farm contractors are supposed to provide drinking water and housing for the workers, but the owners often don't provide water, and the housing may be a shack for an entire family to share.

Sometimes working twelve- to fourteen-hour days in places where the temperature can reach 110 degrees, migrant farmworkers may experience heat-related illnesses, such as dehydration. The Environmental Protection Agency (EPA) and the Occupational Safety and Health Administration (OSHA) estimate approximately 500 deaths occur per year from heat-related illnesses in agricultural fields. Children are more susceptible to heat stress than adults.

Health-Care Assistance for Migrant Farmworkers

People in the UFW, Human Rights Watch, and even some people in the government are working to help improve the health of child and adolescent migrant farmworkers. Captain Evangelina Montoya, a commissioned officer in the U.S. Public Health Service and a former migrant farmworker, is now helping develop health-care policies for migrant farmworkers. In an article on Latina nurses making a difference for migrant farmworkers, she states that when she reads reports on working conditions for farmworkers, "For me it isn't just statistics—it was a fact of life."

Montoya and the Latina nurses say there is a great need for Hispanic nurses. Less than 2 percent of the registered nurse population is of Hispanic descent, and as with teachers, minority populations are more likely to respond positively to advice given from someone who is of their culture, or at least fully understands and respects it.

Farmwork may expose children to harmful chemicals and pesticides.

Organizations such as the National Center for Farmworker Health and the Migrant Clinicians Network exist to specifically address the health-care needs of migrant farmworkers. While these health organizations help improve the health of migrant farmworkers, they are not able to affect policy change at the highest governmental levels. That is what the UFW and Human Rights Watch try to accomplish. For now, these rural youth will continue to work as migrant farmworkers, picking the fruits and vegetables that are distributed throughout the United States and Canada—and dealing with the health implications that go along with their life.

Migrant farmworkers work all over the United States, in three main "streams." The West Coast Stream stretches from southern California to the Pacific Northwest; the Midwest stream starts in Texas and extends north; and the East Coast stream reaches from Florida into Vermont and New Hampshire. The farms that employ migrant workers are often far away from even the smallest villages or towns.

Health Care for Rural Minorities

All rural minorities, not just migrant farmworkers, experience more obstacles to health care than their urban counterparts. The reasons for this vary, from lack of health-care insurance to differences in approach to medical treatment between minority populations and Western medical practitioners.

Overall, however, rural youth minorities do not experience greater health problems than other rural youth or urban minorities. Incidences of asthma, diabetes, and autism are not significantly higher among rural minorities than among urban minorities. However, rural minorities have a harder time than urban minorities

What Are Some Unique Health Care Challenges to Rural Youth Minorities?

In a report by the National Rural Health Association, rural youth minorities must deal with the following obstacles:

- Only about 10 percent of physicians practice in rural America, despite the fact that one-fourth of the population lives in these areas.

- Rural residents are less likely to have employer-provided health care coverage or prescription drug coverage, and the rural poor are less likely to be covered by Medicaid benefits than their urban counterparts.

- Rural minorities tend to be poorer. Nearly 24 percent of rural children live in poverty, much higher than the national average.

- Abuse of alcohol and use of smokeless tobacco is a significant problem among rural youth. Rural eighth graders are twice as likely to smoke cigarettes as students in large urban areas.

- Twenty percent of rural counties lack mental health services versus 5 percent of metropolitan counties.

- The suicide rate among rural male adolescents is significantly higher than in urban areas.

- Medicare payments to rural hospitals and physicians are dramatically less than those to their urban counterparts for equivalent services. This correlates closely with the fact that more than 470 rural hospitals have closed in the past 25 years.

- Rural residents have greater difficulties reaching health care providers, often traveling great distances to reach a doctor or hospital.

in acquiring care for medical services. Many rural hospitals have closed in recent decades, and more rural minorities have no health insurance.

Health advocates such as Montoya hope to see recruitment efforts for minority health-care providers. Other advocates for rural youth minorities are working hard to improve their living conditions as well. Sometimes it is the youth who are themselves doing the work to improve their lives.

CHAPTER 6
Minority Youth Initiatives

Every summer for several years, African American, Native American, and Latino youth have come together at a Youth Land Summit to exchange ideas on minority land issues. The conference brings together young rural minorities who want to learn about each other's cultures and share similar experiences in land-use issues. Participants engage in dialogue and debate about such topics as cooperative community development, *sustainable agriculture*, conflict resolution, land loss and retention, and environmental justice and *reparations*.

When teens combine their talents, they can accomplish much.

An article about the summit in Rural Roots, a community newsletter of the Rural School and Community Trust, reports that the Youth Land Summit began in 2001 and was held at the Federation of Southern Cooperatives' farm in Epes, Alabama. The first year's summit focused on the struggle of communities to retain their farms and land. The next year's gathering took place on the Paiute Nation Reservation in Pyramid Lake, Nevada, and in 2003, a rural Hispanic community in New Mexico hosted the summit.

At each Youth Land Summit, groups of more than forty young people between the ages of fifteen and twenty-three spend a week in each other's communities, learning about land and race issues from the respective native culture. The week includes workshops, speakers, hands-on training, and dialogue and debates about the major land struggles facing minority communities throughout the country. Participants are challenged to think about what they as young people can do about land-control issues and what they can prepare themselves for in the future.

According to the article, the goal of the Youth Land Summit is to "connect the three cultures organizationally and politically using the issues around land as a common lens to look at loss, culture and tradition." Organizers of the summit "hope to reverse the alarming rate of land loss among minority populations and work with community-based organizations to develop alternative enterprises that will permit minority owners to keep their land." The overall belief is that young people are key resources in "expanding land ownership and economic opportunities for people of color in rural communities."

The young people who attend the summit are committed to making a difference in their communities by working toward preserving their respective rural cultures and helping to prevent future loss of cultural traditions through land loss.

In the early twentieth century, the black community owned approximately 19 million acres of rural land. In 1997, African Americans only owned about 2.4 million acres. This represents a vital loss for the rural black community.

Other Youth Initiatives

The prevalence of prejudice and racism throughout the United States and Canada has prompted several youth groups to work for social and political change. One of those groups, the Free Child Project, works to eliminate racism and other social "isms" through education, awareness, and dialogue about community and youth activism. The Free Child Project offers a number of resources through their Web site devoted to help both white and minority youth make a difference in their personal lives and in their larger communities. (You can visit them online at www.freechild.org.)

To include all the people, organizations, and minority youth who are and have been dedicated to making a difference in the lives of rural minorities would more than fill a hundred books this size. We are encouraged by the efforts of César Chávez, who pioneered the fight for migrant farmworkers; Tom Porter, who cofounded the Akwesasne Freedom School; E'Vonne Coleman, who helped make the arts accessible to rural minorities; and the many teachers, nurses, and community leaders who work every day to support and educate rural youth.

USA
37

CESAR E. CHAVEZ

2003

In 2003, the U.S. government put César Chávez's portrait on a stamp to honor his contributions to the lives of migrant workers.

Positive role models can guide rural minority teens toward personal and academic success.

Of course, much remains to be done. Rural minorities continue to encounter barriers to education, health care, work, and land ownership. They also face hate crimes, white supremacist organizations, and structural racism. They need more positive role models from their own communities to help them achieve educational success and to improve their living conditions.

Minorities cannot bring about social change all by themselves. White people have a lot they can learn and a lot they can offer to rural youth minorities. The biggest offering they can make is to take the time to learn about minority cultures and rural issues. Although we will never know, for example, how the young men who murdered James Byrd Jr. may have responded to multicultural education rather than the education they received in prison, we do know that ignorance can only be fought through education and understanding. Through a greater understanding of each other, everyone will have a greater chance to succeed.

Further Reading

Baldwin, James. *The Fire Next Time*. New York: Vintage Books, 2002.

Brown, Dee. *Bury My Heart at Wounded Knee*. New York: Henry Holt, 2001.

Creech, Sharon. *Walk Two Moons*. New York: Harper Trophy, 2004.

Frosch, Mary (editor). *Coming of Age in America: A Multicultural Anthology*. Tarzana, Calif.: Sagebrush, 2005.

Griffin, John Howard. *Black Like Me*. New York: Signet, 2005.

Hamilton, Virginia. *Arilla Sun Down*. New York: Scholastic, 2005.

Jacob, Iris. *My Sister's Voices: Teenage Girls of Color Speak Out*. New York: First Owl Books, 2002.

Kronenwetter, Michael. *Prejudice in America: Causes and Cures*. New York: Franklin Watts, 2003.

Marshall, Joseph M. *The Journey of Crazy Horse: A Lakota History*. New York: Viking Books, 2004.

Mazer, Anne (editor). *America Street: A Multicultural Anthology of Stories*. New York: Persea Books, 2003.

For More Information

American Civil Liberties Union
www.aclu.org

Canadian Rural Partnership: Rural Youth Dialogue
www.rural.gc.ca/dialogue/youth/term_e.phtml

Free Child Project
www.freechild.org/racism.htm

My First Nation's Page
www.eagle.ca/~matink/themes/FirstNations/natives.html

Remembering Jim Crow, Presented by American Radio Works
americanradioworks.publicradio.org/features/remembering

SoundOut.org
www.soundout.org/news.html

Southern Poverty Law Center
www.splcenter.org

Teaching Tolerance
www.tolerance.org

Youth Activism Project
www.youthactivism.com

Youth Policy Action Center
www.youthpolicyactioncenter.org

Publisher's note:
The Web sites listed on this page were active at the time of publication. The publisher is not responsible for Web sites that have changed their addresses or discontinued operation since the date of publication. The publisher will review and update the Web-site list upon each reprint.

Glossary

amenities: Features that, together, make a place attractive.

assimilation: The process by which one group takes on the cultural and other traits of a larger group.

boycott: A joint refusal to buy a certain product or do business at a particular store or chain of stores in order to express disapproval and bring about positive change.

Bureau of Indian Affairs: A department within the U.S. government charged with the oversight of Native American life.

derogatory: Expressing a low opinion of someone or something.

disenfranchise: Deprive a person or organization of a privilege or right, often the right to vote.

emancipation: The act of setting someone free.

hierarchies: Ranks of authority and seniority.

innocuous: Harmless.

insidious: Slowly and subtly harmful.

Jim Crow laws: Laws discriminating against African Americans.

lynchings: The seizing of those believed to have committed a crime and putting them to death, often by hanging.

misnomer: An incorrect or unsuitable name for something or someone.

oppression: The act of imposing a harsh or cruel form of domination.

pension plan: Money paid to a worker after he or she retires.

reparations: Compensation for wrongs.

rites of passage: Ceremonies that mark a person's progress from one stage of life to another.

segregated: Separated from another population.

sharecroppers: Farmers who work the land for the landowner and are paid a share of the crops' yield.

supremacy: The belief that a group of people is better than all others.

sustainable agriculture: A form of farming that keeps the land from being depleted or damaged.

temperate: Not extreme.

unscrupulous: Unrestrained by moral or ethical principles.

upward mobility: The tendency for a person or group of people to move to a higher social or economic level.

Bibliography

Beale, Calvin L. "The Ethno/Racial Context of Poverty and Small Town America." *Poverty and Race*, March/April 2003. http://www.prrac.org/full_text.php?text_id=804&item_id=7806&newsletter_id=67&header=Race+%2F+Racism.

Beswick, Richard. "Racism in America's Schools." ERIC Clearinghouse on Educational Management. Eugene, OR. 1990. http://www.ericdigests.org/pre-9215/racism.htm.

Coleman, E'Vonne. "Balancing Values." Speech given at the University of Massachusetts Amherst on June 28, 2002.

Cromartie, John B. "Minority Counties are Geographically Clustered." *Rural Conditions and Trends* 9, no. 2 (1999): 14–19.

"Fingers to the Bone: Adolescent Farmworkers in the United States: Endangerment and Exploitation." Report by Human Rights Watch, 2000. http://hrw.org/reports/2000/frmwrkr.

Formichelli, Linda. "A Harvest of Hope." 2001. http://www.minoritynurse.com/features/nurse_emp/07-09-01b.html.

http://www.freechild.org

Huang, Gary G. "Sociodemographic Changes: Promise and Problems for Rural Education." ERIC Digest. 1999. http://www.acclaim-math.org/docs/htmlpages/Sociodemographic.htm.

Johnson, Tammy, and Terry Keleher. "Making the Grade: Exposing Structural Racism in Our Schools." *Poverty and Race*, September/October 2001. http://www.prrac.org/full_text.php?text_id=715&item_id=7763&newsletter_id=58&header=Poverty+%2F+Welfare.

Kusimo, Patricia S. "Rural African Americans and Education: The Legacy of the Brown Decision." ERIC Digest. January 1999. http://www.acclaim-math.org/docs/htmlpages/Rural%20Afri%20Americans.htm.

Metz, Andrew. "School Immerses Mohawk Children in Traditional Language." *Newsday*, March 17, 2005. http://mytwobeadsworth.com/Mohawklang31705.html

Miklowitz, Gloria. "Five-Part Series on Cesar Chavez." *Los Angeles Times*, October 3, 2000–October 6, 2000.

Monroe, William. "Time We Moved Beyond Treating Hate's Symptoms." *Houston Chronicle*, June 21, 1998. http://www.chron.com/cs/CDA/ssistory.mpl/special/jasper/reaction/227425.

Pinal, Jorge del, and Audrey Singer. "Generations of Diversity: Latinos in the United States." *Population Bulletin* 52, no. 3 (1997): 1–48.

"Position Statement on Racism, Prejudice, and Discrimination." National Association of School Psychologists, 2004. http://www.nasponline.org/information/pospaper_rpd.html.

Probst, Janice, Charity Moore, Karin Willert Roof, Elizabeth G. Baxley, and Michael E. Samuels. "Access to Care Among Rural Minorities." November 2002. rhr.sph.sc.edu/report/RHRC%20elders%20report.pdf.

"Racism, Violence and Health Project: Calgary Community Forum 2002/2003." Report on the Black Community Forum, Calgary, Alberta, January 25, 2003. http://rvh.socialwork.dal.ca/forum0203cgy.html.

Rowley, Thomas D. "Finding the Funds for Rural Health." *Rural Health News* 8, no. 1 (Spring 2001).

Smith, Andrea. "Soul Wound: The Legacy of Native American Schools." Amnesty, 2005. http://www.amnestyusa.org/amnestynow/soulwound.html.

Summers, Gene. "Race and Rural Poverty." *Poverty and Race*, January/February 1997. http://www.prrac.org/full_text.php?text_id=274&item_id=2824&newsletter_id=30&header=Race+%2F+Racism

"Taking Stock: Rural People, Poverty, and Housing at the Turn of the 21st Century." Housing Assistance Center, 2002. http://www.ruralhome.org/pubs/hsganalysis/ts2000/executivesummary.htm.

"The Trail of Tears." http://www.historicaldocuments.com/indianremovalact.htm.

U.S. Department of Health and Human Services. "Mental Health: Culture, Race, Ethnicity: Report of the Surgeon General." Washington, D.C.: Author, 1999. http://www.mentalhealth.samhsa.gov/cre/default.asp.

Williams, Doris Terry, and Jereann King. *Rural School Leadership in the Deep South: The Double-Edged Legacy of School Desegregation*. Washington, D.C.: The Rural School Community Trust, 2002.

Index

Picture Credits

Harding House Publishing, Ben Stewart: pp. 35, 36, 39, 57, 66, 82
iStockphoto: pp. 21, 68
    Baumgartner, Betty: p. 22
    Brandenburg, Dan: p. 44
    Comeau, Ronnie: p. 61
    Estey, Juan: p. 10
    Gough, Lawrence: p. 54
    Gumerov, Oleksandr: p. 52
    Hart, Eileen: pp. 8, 43
    Louie, Nancy: p. 50
    Memory, Jelani: p. 40
    Monu, Nicholas: p. 17
    Nehring, Nancy: p. 76
    Russ, Kevin: p. 24
    Walker, Duncan: p. 15
Jupiter Images: pp. 71, 72, 80, 86
Library and Archives Canada: p. 27
Library of Congress: pp. 31, 49, 58
McIntosh, Kenneth: pp. 13, 18, 28, 64
National Archives and Records Administration: pp. 33, 47
U.S. Postal Service: p. 85

To the best knowledge of the publisher, all other images are in the public domain. If any image has been inadvertently uncredited, please notify Harding House Publishing Service, Vestal, New York 13850, so that rectification can be made for future printings.

Biographies

Author

Elizabeth Bauchner lives in Ithaca, New York, with her three children. She enjoys writing about many topics, including health, politics, sociology, and biology. In 2005, her book *What Do I Have to Lose? A Teen's Guide to Weight Management* was released by Mason Crest Publishers. She has also written *Computer Investigation and Document Analysis* for Mason Crest.

Series Consultant

Celeste J. Carmichael is a 4-H Youth Development Program Specialist at the Cornell University Cooperative Extension Administrative Unit in Ithaca, New York. She provides leadership to statewide 4-H Youth Development efforts including communications, curriculum, and conferences. She communicates the needs and impacts of the 4-H program to staff and decision makers, distributing information about issues related to youth and development, such as trends for rural youth.